Morning 1808

Morning 1808

Boston Harbor

A Novel by Shirley M. Sprague

MORNING 1808
BOSTON HARBOR

Copyright © 2014 Shirley M. Sprague.

All rights reserved. No part of this book may be used or reproduced by any means, graphic, electronic, or mechanical, including photocopying, recording, taping or by any information storage retrieval system without the written permission of the publisher except in the case of brief quotations embodied in critical articles and reviews.

iUniverse books may be ordered through booksellers or by contacting:

iUniverse
1663 Liberty Drive
Bloomington, IN 47403
www.iuniverse.com
1-800-Authors (1-800-288-4677)

Because of the dynamic nature of the Internet, any web addresses or links contained in this book may have changed since publication and may no longer be valid. The views expressed in this work are solely those of the author and do not necessarily reflect the views of the publisher, and the publisher hereby disclaims any responsibility for them.

Any people depicted in stock imagery provided by Thinkstock are models, and such images are being used for illustrative purposes only.
Certain stock imagery © Thinkstock.

ISBN: 978-1-4917-4200-6 (sc)
ISBN: 978-1-4917-4201-3 (e)

Library of Congress Control Number: 2014915194

Printed in the United States of America.

iUniverse rev. date: 8/28/2014

Preface

Before moving to college level teaching, I worked with accelerated high school students, most of them planning for college. They were wonderfully inquisitive groups, willing workers with questions about everything. Many enjoyed literature with mystery and the use of occult or death themes. They enjoyed Poe's stories and poetry and were drawn to his unusual background. Where was he born? What happened to his parents? They were actors!? They often asked to do individual extra credit reports. In their work they were very thorough and noticed any discrepancy of time or place.

This led me to further research at Kent during my pursuit of a master's degree. Kent has a very good twelve-story library full of outstanding reference material. The reference page, following the last chapter of this book, illustrates the wide span of years of my various literary sources.

Research for the book was pursued as nonfiction, a true situation, but some of the crucial evidence from 200 years ago was destroyed. This book explains why the truth can never be proven as it stands currently. Edgar was born January 19, 1809. His conception, then, would have been in the early spring of 1808. Thus, my title <u>Morning 1808</u>. I truly believe that John Howard Payne was the father of Edgar Allan Poe.

So, Dear Reader, consider the evidence and decide for yourself.

Acknowlegements

In memory of my husband, Sid Sprague.
With appreciation to Karen Sprague, who spent
many hours in technical preparation,
and
To my mentors in the English Department at Kent State University.

"A mystery, and a dream, should my early life seem."
Edgar Allan Poe

Contents

Preface v
Acknowlegements vii
Introduction xiii

Chapter 1   Boston Arrival
               January 3, 1796 1
Chapter 2   In Boston 1796 5
Chapter 3   Night at the Waterfront 7
Chapter 4   On Tour 1797 11
Chapter 5   Aftermath 15
Chapter 6   John at the Grant + Forbes Counting House 21
Chapter 7   At Union College
               1806-1808 25
Chapter 8   Return to Boston
               1806-1809 33
Chapter 9   A Very Memorable Weekend 39
Chapter 10 The First American Hamlet 41
Chapter 11 Summer in Baltimore 1809 49
Chapter 12 Alone 55
Chapter 13 Finale 59
Chapter 14 John Howard in Washington and Abroad 61

Rationale 63
Source References 67
Selection of Poems by
John Howard Payne 69
About the Author: 75

Introduction

The Encounter

What was going on downstairs in the costume storage rooms? Betty moved down the hall closer to the stairwell to catch a glimpse of the men who were busy looking over the racks of "dresses," as the actors called the stage outfits and the boxes of hats and props accompanying them. Betty recognized the voice of Mr. Powell talking to another man who seemed to be in charge of two boys who scurried back and forth loading the wagon outside on the street.

Straining to get a better view through the open door, and curious about all the activity, she was greeted by an attractive, curly haired boy about her age who had just come upstairs and was standing there smiling at her.

"Good morning! Hope I didn't frighten you. My father sent me upstairs to find an empty crate somewhere. You're with the troupe of London actors which arrived yesterday, aren't you?"

"Yes, I am. Last season Mr. Powell played opposite my mother at the Theater Royal in Covent Gardens and invited her and her troupe to go to America for their first engagement here at the 1796 winter season of the Boston Federal Theater," Betty said proudly, "and she is allowing me to sing a number after the play's main performance."

Betty stopped short, suddenly remembering what her mother had told her to say. "And besides that, I'm only nine years old."

"Nine years old," John laughed. "I can plainly see that you are <u>more</u> than nine years old!"

"How can you plainly see that?" Betty challenged.

"I can plainly see how your blouse fits you!" John said with a devilish smile.

"Don't you talk that way to me. Go downstairs and help your father! Stop bothering me now!"

"I'm sorry, but you did ask. Don't be angry. I'll look forward to hearing you sing. I often come to the Theater."

"Why is your father looking through the storage boxes with Mr. Powell?" Betty questioned.

"My father is headmaster at Berry Street Academy not far from the Theater. We are presenting a program on the school stage and Mr. Powell is lending us some dresses for the performance."

"That sounds like fun. Your father must be a very good headmaster to be able to manage an academy and also produce theater programs. My mother says it is necessary to be very careful, as stage performances must not offend the religious church people living in Boston."

"Well, my father does his best to please everyone, but it's not easy," John offered. "But you haven't mentioned your father. I heard that he was also an actor at Convent Gardens. Is he here with the troupe?"

"No, he and my mother were stars at the Theater Royal, but he was stabbed to death late one night in a pub fight with a jealous actor. I was born five months later—and I know what you are thinking. My poor mother had to live through ugly gossip about the morals of actresses, but he was my father and they were married, and she is a fine lady."

"Yes, yes, your momma's a fine lady (more seriously speaking)," John agreed. "Many people are very cruel to actresses for no reason."

"He died years ago and nothing can change it now," Betty said. "I must go now and rehearse my song."

"Yes, I hear my father calling me. Would you like to visit our academy on Berry Street and meet my big family? There is never Theater nor school on Sunday, only Sabbath duties and meditation for the pious. I could come to the nearby house where Mr. Powell always boards his acting troupe to meet you in the afternoon. It's not far from here," said John.

Betty was pleased. "I'd like to see your academy and meet your family, but I don't even know your name—and how do you know where actors <u>always</u> stay?"

"I always know about what is happening in the Theater. I'll see you Sunday afternoon, Miss Betty Arnold." He said her name with emphasis. "My name is John Howard Payne, and Betty, someday I'm going to be an actor, too."

Chapter 1

Boston Arrival
January 3, 1796

When <u>The Outram</u> embarked on its journey to America in November 1795, the departing passengers included a group of actors who had been hired by Mr. Charles Stuart Powell for the reopening of the Federal Street Theater in Boston. Mr. Powell hoped for a good season, since in recent years, circumstances were not always advantageous. Stage presentations in the theater had been legally approved in both Boston and Philadelphia in 1793, but still shunned by the Puritans: therefore, the judicial decree was slow to gain general acceptance.

After the failure of the new Exhibition Room in 1793, Mr. Powell had built the next year "a handsome two story brick edifice with a columned portico" which opened February 3, 1794 with the American play, <u>Gustavus Vasa</u>. He was disappointed by bankruptcy at the end of the season. Even attempts to disguise plays as "edifying lessons for moral justification" had not always met with success. Sometimes actors had to endure public censure, possibly whipping as punishment for "sinful actions".

Discouraged by the failure of the opening season of 1794 at his newly built Federal Street Theater, Mr. Powell sailed to England, where theater flourished, hoping to learn from theater method and operation abroad. At the Theater Royal in Covent Gardens, he appeared often with Mrs. Elizabeth Arnold who was a popular actress on the London stage. Tall and attractive, she had begun a successful career in 1791. Her husband Henry Arnold had also been an actor at Covent Gardens, but was killed in a pub fight with a jealous actor in the winter of 1787. His wife continued on stage starting with small vocal parts, but her roles increased in importance soon. Mr. Powell returned to America encouraged by his London experience and before leaving, engaged Mrs. Arnold and her troupe to come to Boston for the upcoming season at the Federal State Theater.

When the time came in November for its trip to America, the Theater troupe hired by Mr. Powell boarded The Outram ready to start a new life and new career. The troupe included Mrs. Elizabeth Arnold along with her daughter, Betty, Miss Alice Green and Charley Tubbs, a musician as well as actor. It was a small but talented and capable group. At that time, one actor played a number of roles. They had been assured that it would be possible to locate other compatible actors to complete the troupe, if they were needed.

During the two months aboard ship on the ocean voyage, they made good use of the time to prepare for their first American appearance. There was work to do besides revising and rehearsing the scripts which would have to be more conservative than those played in England. When the sea was calm enough, the costumes were mended or altered as suitable for all plays, and all props were mended and others prepared. Mr. Powell had suggested that the costumes or dresses as they were called in Theater circles would be a real asset as many American troupes did not have appropriate clothing and props for the play time period to enhance the performance. Also during the voyage, Mrs. Arnold and Charley Tubbs decided to marry upon arrival in Boston. They had been friends for years in London although a marriage for mutual convenience was not uncommon then as now.

On the morning of January 3, 1796, The Outram docked in Boston Harbor. The English passengers, hearing all the landing activity, hurried to the top deck to see what was happening. The Outram was

Morning 1808

surrounded by other ships with sailors unloading cargo from faraway places to be sold to Boston merchants. Betty wondered what could be in all those boxes and crates—many small and others so bulky that two or three sailors had to maneuver them safely down the ramp to dockside. Mr. Powell was among the group at the dock, while <u>The Outram</u> passengers disembarked. As they carefully walked down the swaying ramp to the solid dock, Mr. Powell warmly greeted each troupe member. They were soon on their way to the Federal Street Theater with their baggage in tow on a wagon. They were anxious to see the boarding house where they would live while in Boston. For Betty and the group a new life began.

Chapter 2

In Boston 1796

The new Federal Street Theater was modern for 1796, patterned after London playhouses and the English troupe felt quite at home. Plays were scheduled for Monday/Wednesday/Friday allowing play choice from their repertoire and rehearsal time. Tickets were available for sale at local taverns for the prime seats at seven shillings, a lesser price according to location in the Theater or gallery. When the doors opened at 5:00 p.m., servants often were sent to reserve the best seats for their wealthy masters. Seating could accommodate possibly 700 people and ranged from lower floor seats, a horseshoe tier of boxes lining the stage from side to side, the prime seats for hearing and viewing perception. General and least costly seating was in the above large gallery. Unfortunately for the actors, the loud, rowdy behavior of "patrons" in the gallery, during this early period in America, taunted the actors at times by shouting rude comments or pelting them with popcorn, peanuts or other missiles bought outside the Theater door. Candlelight was the only available lighting. Many candlelit chandeliers were hung in central locations, more in brackets attached to the front of each box with as many as possible in individual candleholders completely lining the stage on the proscenium which served as the stage apron. The musicians were seated in a reserved section directly in front of the stage. They too needed the candlelight.

The necessity to use candle lighting after dark, in homes as well as public buildings such as theaters, presented a constant danger. Many Christmas trees so decorated would go up in flames no matter how carefully attended by the family often causing the home to burn to the ground also. With the Theater stage needing the light for actor visibility and clarity of performance, play action was most effective down stage very close to the candles. Many Theaters were completely destroyed by an upset candle somewhere in the Theater, afire and engulfing the Theater too quickly out of control. A tragic example of this common hazard is recorded in theatrical annals.

On the night of December 26, 1811 at a gala performance attended by the Governor of Virginia, the magnificent brick Richmond Theater burned to ashes. The play in progress was <u>The Bleeding Nun</u> performed by Placide's company to a packed house. Seventy-two people died that night, including the Governor of Virginia.

The Burning of the theater in Richmond, Virginia
on the Night of December 26, 1811.

Chapter 3

Night at the Waterfront

Soon the troupe was unpacked and ready for opening night. As customary, a handbill was distributed throughout town announcing the grand opening of the new season. When the night arrived and the doors opened, the Theater filled quickly with people curious to see these English strangers on stage and listen to their alien way of pronunciation. Mr. Powell was delighted. At exactly 6:30, he walked to center stage and, as standard Theater procedure, rang the bell which announced that the play would begin. He also had a shrill whistle commonly used by some managers, but tonight was important. He rang the bell with vigor!

Mrs. Arnold (still her stage name) elegant and slender, wearing just the right style dress, made her debut as Rosetta in the comic opera <u>Love in a Village</u>. It was February 16, 1796 and the troupe was happy to be in America.

An article soon appeared in the local newspaper, <u>The Massachusetts Mercury,</u> announcing the arrival of the talented Theater troupe from London. The reporter noted that both Mrs. Arnold and Miss Green were "tall and genteel and moved with symmetry unequalled while maintaining an expressive countenance." As her mother had promised, Betty made her first appearance on the Federal Street Theater stage singing the currently popular song "The Market Lass."

She was accompanied by pianoforte player Mr. Charley Tubbs, her new stepfather. Her mother had included Betty's special performance as a tribute to a very receptive audience on her first benefit night.

As he had promised Betty in the Theater hallway the day after the arrival of her group, John took her for a tour of the Berry Street Academy and introduced her to his family. This was the first of many hours they would spend together. In a short time, Betty learned that John was not only precocious even though he was younger than she, but also had a reputation of being wild and recalcitrant. He enjoyed roaming the Boston waterfront when the sailors, from many countries, were on shore leave from all the ships docked in the harbor from time to time. He confided in Betty that he not only enjoyed the afternoon visits to the waterfront, but he often would sneak out at night after curfew. His father forbid these escapades without much luck. Betty enjoyed the afternoon walks with John to the bustling harbor. It was exciting to watch the tall-masted ships arriving with cargo to be unloaded or departing for some far-off destination. She found herself now and then dreaming of getting on a ship like the ones docked in Boston Harbor, and traveling to exotic places so different from Boston, maybe even dressed like some of the foreign travelers she had noticed leaving <u>The Outram</u>. And now she had met John. If they were together, life would be exciting no matter where they traveled.

John wanted her to go along with him on the night excursions, too, although Betty knew her mother would absolutely not approve. John was very persuasive. Finally against her better judgment, she occasionally accompanied him late at night to watch the harbor night-time action—very different from daytime activity. John had noticed an abandoned nearby storage building, which he had been using on his previous trips at night to the waterfront alone. He and Betty discreetly watched all the activity of the sailors and local people who roamed the area, and Betty learned of an exciting world that she never imagined had existed. Very soon she realized John's reputation was well-deserved.

Morning 1808

As it turned out, Betty was very happy that her mother and the troupe had accepted Mr. Powell's invitation for them to come to Boston. She had liked him last year when he was in London on stage with her mother. Everyone was very excited that they had come to America. At first Betty was nervous, never knowing any Americans except Mr. Powell. Most people in London thought all Americans were cowboys, but Mr. Powell said that wasn't true.

As the weeks passed, more and more people were attending the plays. It was a very successful season, and everyone even liked her songs. She could hardly wait for her mother to allow her to act on stage—even if she were only given minor character roles at first.

After enduring previous season failure and bankruptcy, Mr. Powell finally had achieved success with his newly-erected Federal Street Theater. He was also very pleased with Boston's response to the English acting troupe. It had been well worth his trip to London to find them. Box office receipts and attendance increased week after week throughout the entire season.

John was disappointed when Betty told him that her mother had decided that they would be leaving Boston, when the season was over, to locate summer Theater opportunities. She promised him that she would write to him when she could—postal service was not always available and, at best, very slow. However, a number of years would pass before they would be together again.

Chapter 4

On Tour 1797

When the season ended, Betty accompanied her parents and the troupe on a their first tour. (For Betty, the season had ended too soon.) It was necessary for acting troupe to go south during the off-season to look for play opportunities there. This summer would be their first summer season, and Betty had overheard their uncertain attempts at mapping a suitable course. She knew from discussion that staging would not be as nice as they had enjoyed in Boston. They settled briefly in Portland, Maine.

Plays in the south were often performed in remodeled barns—and sometimes not even remodeled barns. The audiences usually were very small, since most people lived in widely separated areas. But the troupe needed ongoing financial support. Betty couldn't imagine a play acted in a barn with animals there. And besides, most of all, she was going to miss John.

Mrs. Arnold was aware that Betty was very unhappy, and to give her something positive in her life, suggested that maybe it was time for Betty to try more important roles. It was just what Betty needed! She was allowed to choose, for her first appearance, to play Biddy Bellair in Gerrick's <u>Miss in Her Teens</u>. No actress had ever more carefully prepared for a first major appearance.

Betty's career was formally launched on November 17, 1796 when she was an opening night success as Biddy. The critics from the <u>Eastern Herald and Gazette of Maine</u> had this to write about her performance:

"Her power as an actress would do credit to any of her mature age."

But he added a further warning for ladies to avoid theater unless they were certain that "their ears would not be offended by expressions of obscenity and profanity."

It's possible that "adventurous" ladies might just have been moved to attend the Theater out of curiosity after reading his admonition against what might be experienced.

Although Mrs. Arnold and Betty are all but ignored in early Theater records, their careers can often be traced through newspaper records and old playbills still in existence. According to the Massachusetts Mercury account when they played in Boston, Mrs. Arnold gave her age as 24 and her daughter's as nine years. Other conflicting dates suggest that she took some liberty with the truth to preserve her youthful image. However, Betty had been unable to convince John that she was nine years old at their first meeting.

The family group, Betty with her parents, left Portland (a poor first choice) due to the extremely cold weather there, plus further financial reverses, and joined John Sollee briefly at New York's John Street Theater with a sojourn in Philadelphia. Again Betty was favorably received by audiences. "Her youth, beauty and innocence astonished and delighted the public." Further reports noted that she had "a sylph-like grace with a face framed in curls and a small delicate figure."

After a successful season in Philadelphia, John Sollee and company moved south in the spring of 1798 to Charleston. Unfortunately with summer arriving, the constant threat of a yellow fever outbreak soon developed. Never having lived in a tropical climate, the English actor family had not experienced an epidemic of this kind. Added to this disadvantage, a major controversy developed between Mr. Sollee and actors in the larger group. The three men, one of whom was Charley Tubbs, felt Mr. Sollee had not allotted the right of benefit nights fairly among all troupe members. Since actors were financially insecure often, all of them monitored Mr. Sollee's assignment of benefits to each player. The benefit system, used at the discretion of the manager, provided that, on a given evening, an actor would receive the profits for the performance after all the expenses were paid. However, if the receipts were less than the expenses for the performance, the actor would be required to make up the losses. The discussion became very heated and Mr. Sollee referred to Charley Tubbs as "a vermin." Immediately Mr. Tubbs gathered his loyal forces to form the Charleston players, who set out on their own shortly thereafter. The Yellow Fever outbreak developed into a raging epidemic. The Church St. Theater in Charleston was forced to close.

Heading for a promise of engagement in Philadelphia with the Wignell New Theater Company on Oct 20, 1797, Mrs. Arnold contacted an old friend from London, Nellie Snowdon, who joined their troupe for this Philadelphia season. They also added Charles Hopkins, a comedian and Luke Noble Usher, a Shakespearian player. The expanded company was well-received in Philadelphia at the Walnut St. Theater with The Wignall Company, who had lost several of their actors in the yellow fever epidemic. But tragedy was to come. Before leaving Charleston, Charlie Tubbs began to feel the symptoms of yellow fever which was widespread in Charleston. Before long, because yellow fever is very contagious, Mrs. Arnold, sharing his bed, eventually was infected also. Sorely needing the money, Mrs. Arnold continued to act even in a feverish weakened condition. On January 11, 1799, in M. G. Lewis' <u>Castle Specter</u> she appeared as Angela with Luke Usher as Lord Reginald, his first major role with the company. The play was one of her favorites, a difficult role as Angela in which she is accosted by apparitions and ghostly villains. By the third act, she was very weak and delirious with fever. Moving downstage, she cried out:

"Begone wretched apparition!"

"Take thy form from my sight.!"

"Cold wrath! I do not fear thy evil wail!"

As she passionately turned to face away to the audience, in her delirium she moved far too close to the edge of the stage proscenium. Her long full skirt brushed over top the closest candle. Though rigid in its holder, the candle flame leaped to touch the hem of her skirt. In a moment, fingers of red and yellow flames climbed her dress and to her elaborate head piece. She became a live raging torch. Horrified by the sight, Luke Usher rushed to her side, carrying a wall-hanging curtain prop. Using it like a blanket, he wrapped up her body and pushed her to the stage floor. With the help of the other actors on stage, they smothered the fire. Luke had saved the Theater, but Mrs. Arnold was in grave danger, writhing in agony and complete shock.

Mrs. Arnold died during the night, January 12, 1799. Overcome with grief at the loss of his wife as well as the worsening effects of his own illness, Charley Tubbs died one week later.

They were interred side by side in a potter's grave in Philadelphia, a common practice at that time for transient persons without local family financial support.

Chapter 5

Aftermath

Betty was devastated at the age of fourteen; she had lost her precious mother, who had suffered a painful, miserable death. After coming to Boston, when Betty had begun to perform in minor stage roles, Mrs. Arnold had warned her to avoid moving too close to the row of candles surrounding the stage. It was a bitter irony that she, in her feverish delirium, should succumb to that very danger. Betty also grieved for Charley Tubbs, the only father figure she had ever known. For only those few years, he had been kind and helpful, always building her confidence as he accompanied her on the pianoforte while she sang.

But Betty was not alone in grief. Nellie Snowden immediately came to her as a protective friend. Betty also was grateful to Luke Usher who had tried in vain to save her mother.

Unknown to most of the actors in Wignell's New Theater Company, Luke Usher had followed Nellie Snowden when he learned that she had joined Wignell's Troupe. Although she had been attracted to him the year before, Luke had fallen deeply in love with her. But she had refused when he proposed to her. Her first marriage to Ben Snowden was a happy one at first, but his unreasonable jealousy soon made living together a nightmare. After the divorce, he disappeared.

Mrs. Elizabeth Arnold, who knew of their problems, finally had convinced her that she should try to put the past behind her. Recalling her encouragement, Nellie accepted Luke's proposal and they married in the spring of 1799. Betty now felt confident in being looked after by both Mr. and Mrs. Usher.

Elizabeth Arnold Poe

Many years later Edgar Allan Poe honored the kindness to his mother, Elizabeth, using the Usher name in one of his greatest short stories. "The Fall of the House of Usher" still is studied in many American Literature text books used currently in high school throughout America.

The Ushers and Elizabeth (no longer Betty) still with Wignell and Company played in the Baltimore season in 1799. Betty was cast for the first time on Oct 4, 1799 in the major role of Molly Maybush, the rural maid in O'Keefe's <u>The Farmer</u>. Later when the occasion was announced, Thomas Wignell as manager and his company were awarded the honor of opening the first Theater in Washington on August 22, 1800. In the afterpiece, Elizabeth played her popular role as Little Pickle in <u>The Spoiled Child</u>, a part she did particularly well with her petite figure and winsome manner. But it was a short summer season which closed September 19.

The fall season at the Chestnut Street Theater proved very successful for Elizabeth and the Ushers, who appeared regularly in many roles in the popular plays of the period. The season enjoyed a full run and closed April 19, 1801.

Elizabeth's first important Shakespearean role as Ophelia in <u>Hamlet</u> was performed in the old Southwick Theater on September 23, 1801. The Theater had reopened for the summer season of 1801 in Philadelphia. This was a demanding role for a fourteen year old girl, but her performance rated a favorable review by newspaper critics. The weekly play continued to be popular and the season ran through the spring of 1802. On April 7, 1802, Elizabeth shared a benefit with Luke and Nellie Usher in Morton's <u>Speed the Plough</u>. A new actor had joined Thomas Wignell Company by this time. A popular comedian, Charles Hopkins, was an instant success with his opening performance as the character of "Tony Lumpkin". This added a new promising dimension to the troupe. During the season Elizabeth shared the stage with Charles Hopkins in various plays and in off-stage time as well.

He was a likeable and kind young fellow. With his keen sense of humor, he could make Elizabeth laugh and, little by little, help her regain her happy outlook on life. He told her that he was sure that her mother would not approve of her sad depression. Elizabeth soon shared his affection and came to realize that, even though the Ushers were protective friends, marriage with Charles would bring mutual love and complete security. They exchanged marriage vows during the summer of 1802.

Shortly after their marriage, the Hopkins left the Wignell Company to join Green's Virginia Company. For the next two years they moved from city to city—Charleston, Baltimore, Philadelphia, Norfolk, and Richmond—wherever could be found a playhouse and a fair audience. Both Mr. and Mrs. Hopkins were gaining popularity and receiving good press notices. She appeared in 21 different parts with her singing talent much in demand. They were both very young, Elizabeth in her middle to late teens.

In the spring of 1804, Mr. and Mrs. Hopkins met David Poe in Richmond and they played together in a Theater/barn which had been converted from its original use after a great fire. Theaters in the south were often make-shift with little seating area.

David Poe was a handsome, dashing young man who had been studying to become a lawyer as his parents had hoped, but he left school at nineteen to pursue acting. Not very talented and often panned by the critics, he was defensive and often belligerent about criticism. He had been known to go looking for the critic who ridiculed his acting with a horse whip. But he was stage-struck and had left his uncle's home in Augusta, Georgia despite warning of the family. Cast in secondary roles or minor walk-on parts, the audience seemed to be kind to him at first because of his handsome appearance. But his amateurish performance noted by the critics was his undoing.

David felt most comfortable playing Shakespearean roles especially as a young lover. He told Elizabeth that he had seen her in 1802 on the stage at Baltimore and talked to her backstage after the performance that evening. She didn't remember.

After trouble developed in the company, Charles Hopkins took over the management and both Charles and Elizabeth along with David appeared regularly on stage in old favorite plays and new ones. As David slowly improved, he often played lead roles opposite Elizabeth. Under Charles Hopkins's management, the troupe was strengthened in stage presentation as well as renewed group cooperation. But it had been a difficult worrisome rebuilding period for Charles Hopkins.

During the summer of 1805, he developed a chronic dry cough which caused sleepless nights, although he tried hard to hide the increasing symptoms from Elizabeth. However as the weeks passed, Elizabeth knew she was losing him. No available medical treatment they sought was of help. Charles Hopkins died on October 26, 1805. (His death was reported in <u>The Virginia Gazette</u> in Richmond. This was evidence of the respect he had attained in the city as actors were seldom considered important figures.) They had shared just three very happy but very short years together in marriage. Another crushing experience for Elizabeth. But in the six years since her mother's death, she had matured in many ways. She was able to cope a little better with misfortune, gratified at least for their short, but wonderful times together as man and wife.

Three weeks later, a letter from John Howard Payne was delivered to her. She hadn't heard from him for a long time. As Elizabeth had promised John Howard before leaving with her parents for the Portland engagement, she wrote to him and whenever the troupe was playing for a full winter season, he would also write to her at that location. However, when Mrs. Arnold became aware that they were corresponding, it temporarily ended. Mrs. Arnold did not approve of their friendship.

She had learned in Portland of Betty's night escapades to the Boston Harbor with John. They had been seen by a Boston dock worker, who also had been a backstage hand at the Federal Street Theater earlier that year. Confronted by her mother, Betty had confessed. Although her mother forbade any further letters, Betty continued writing occasionally whenever she could. John, who was a master at all kinds of connivance, handled it well.

Although Elizabeth had stopped writing to him after she married Charlie Hopkins, she was pleased to receive this letter. He had heard of Charles Hopkins' death from Richmond friends living in New York and offered his condolences. John currently was employed in a counting house in New York, but was still determined to pursue an acting career. Another stage struck young man. It was now a little easier for them to correspond, but not entirely, since Mr. Payne thought Elizabeth, the actress, was a very negative influence on his son and disapproved of their friendship. A career in accounting to him was much more preferable to a transient life of poverty as an actor.

Elizabeth, the Ushers and David Poe continued to play in Green's Company in Richmond when the fall/winter season opened. They were well received with the good reputation they now enjoyed in Richmond. David Poe, who had never forgotten Elizabeth since meeting her in Boston backstage in 1802, was always at her side to help her in any way he could.

Now she appeared opposite David on stage frequently. On November 6 in a benefit for her, Elizabeth played Julia Clairville to David's Mandeville in Cumberland's play <u>The Sailor's Daughter</u>. Lead roles continued for them in material they had used successfully such as Elizabeth as Lady Randolph and David as Norval in <u>Douglas</u> by Holme. They also added some Shakespearean tragedy in <u>Macbeth</u> late in the season. Although Elizabeth grieved for Charles, she was aware that David was falling in love with her. In March, he proposed to her and they were married on April 5, 1806. He was 22; she was 18. Just five months had passed since Charles' death, but Elizabeth had learned that life must go on and marriage to a handsome young man would be both desirable and expedient under her circumstances.

When the season was over in the spring, Mr. and Mrs. Poe left Richmond and the Virginia Company with plans to meet the Ushers in the fall. Through family contacts, David had made arrangements for them to act in the summer Theater at Vauxhall Gardens in New York City, a very different and more professional engagement for them. When fall came, they would reunite with the Ushers in Boston.

Chapter 6

John at the Grant + Forbes Counting House

When they left Richmond, Elizabeth wrote to John of their plans to be in New York that summer and then to Boston that fall. John laughed aloud as he read Elizabeth's letter and then he read it again. Finally they would be together as he had promised her years ago. He had not seen her since she left for Portland in 1797 with her family. He too would be in New York during the summer and certainly would attend the summer Theater in Vaux Hall Gardens to see her on stage. Furthermore, he would be at home in Boston for a visit with family before starting his college term. They had so much to tell each other. He hoped that her new husband would understand that Elizabeth and he were old friends from the past, long before she knew him.

As he started a letter to her with the good news, all the happy memories flooded his mind. They had had so much fun together while her family was performing at the Boston Federal Street Theater and he was attending his father's Berry Street Academy nearby. He paused in writing as he recalled their visits to the Boston Harbor, both afternoon and night—especially the night escapades. He wished that she could have been there to act with him in the academy productions during those next years. He wanted to share with her the invitation he had received to tour with an acting group. Of course his father refused to let him go with them. Mr. Payne reminded John that acting was only a pleasant past-time—not a money-making career. Furthermore, John was too young. But of course long ago, John had decided otherwise. As he told Elizabeth (Betty then), he had always planned to be an actor.

Finances were always a problem for Mr. Payne. With nine children to feed and clothe and academy responsibilities, Mr. Payne counted on his sons to help as they grew older. He had been successful in securing a position for William, his oldest son, age 20, to work as a clerk in a counting house in New York. However, William had always battled poor health and the following year he died of consumption, later to be known as tuberculosis. William's work had been exemplary and Mr. Forbes contacted Mr. Payne thinking his second oldest son, John, might be able to fill the position. Obviously he had never met John, but Mr. Payne was delighted with the opportunity offered to him. Even though John was not quite fifteen, he replaced his older brother as a mercantile clerk in the counting house of Grant and Forbes September 1805 to help support his family. His parents hoped to divert him from his passion for a stage career. Equally important, they needed the money.

Although dreading the "boring" job assigned to him, and away from home and family for the first time, John's self-assurance soon made him become aware of the opportunity surrounding him. Unlike his brother William, he had other interests besides working long hours as an accounting clerk. John was charming, good looking, with blue eyes and curly blond hair, very creative, intelligent and gifted in Theater production as well as acting. But as the years passed, he would make many enemies, since he also was extravagant, not good with finances and always in debt.

John was impressed that New York had become a growing city, no longer a small town with a rural atmosphere. He remembered when they had lived there, before moving to Boston and the Berry Street Academy. John enjoyed strolling down Broadway with the new street lamps, many lovely homes everywhere, a new water works system (rather than pumps) with a piping system installed. But as exciting as John found the city, his job proved to be dull and tedious for twelve hours, six days a week. He spent these long hours sitting in silence on a high hard stool, hour after hour, day after day. The owner/supervisor, R. B. Forbes, stern and cold to him, was also very demanding. At six o'clock quitting time, he walked

Morning 1808

to Pearl Street to the boarding house where he stayed with a number of other boarders. He cringed at their irritating jokes and conversation. They called him "Jack"—which they knew he hated.

John had found the Park Theatre[1] on Park Row! Unfortunately he had little money to spend and his long working hours cut into the evening performances starting at 6:30 p.m. But John still enjoyed being there whenever possible.

By December, he was very unhappy with his work place. Mr. Forbes had forbidden entertainment and even objected to his reading the newspaper accounts of theatre happenings. Without Mr. Forbes' knowledge, John made visits backstage and successfully secured a possible stage appearance. Mr. Payne absolutely forbid this when John told him of the opportunity when home for Christmas, even though John claimed it would pay well. To Mr. Payne, a full-time steady position was more important.

To overcome his frustration and boredom, John turned to writing a newspaper <u>The Thespian Mirror</u> late at night in his room. The first issue appeared in the N.Y. newsstands on 12/29/1805. He had completed it in three days after returning to N. Y. disappointed by his father's negative reaction to the theatre acting offer.

His little magazine/newspaper was a great success with New Yorkers. They enjoyed the unusual nature of his little creation. All about theatre, the purpose of the small eight-page issue was to promote interest in American drama. As further issues appeared, few people knew that the editor was not quite fifteen years old. However, as precocious as John was, this did not stand in his way. He began receiving mail from his readers. He even developed the friendship of well-known and well-to-do local people, such as Henry Brevoort, who introduced John to his friend, Washington Irving. Very soon, John gained the attention of William Coleman, the editor of <u>The Evening Post</u>. Impressed by his young age, Mr. Coleman thought John should go to college. Of course, his employer Mr. Forbes made every effort to squelch that suggestion and his family disapproved, fearing that such a stressful life at college might cause an illness. But Mr. Coleman ignored

---

1   In time the Theaters merited a more exclusive spelling—"theater" became "theatre"—by becoming more accepted and elaborate.

all objections and, as The Thespian Mirror continued to appear weekly, John's possible college attendance was investigated. Finally, Mr. John E. Seaman, a respected local merchant, was selected as John's benefactor. Mr. Seaman had been a friend of John's brother William while he lived in New York and was well-impressed with William's younger sibling. He had even considered adopting John. However, with college plans in place, John was finally persuaded to give up The Thespian Mirror in order to give his full attention to college. The last edition was published March 22, 1806.

During his literary adventure of The Thespian Mirror, John was also writing his first play late at night, while working at Forbes counting house each day. On the basis of the public's approval of his literary work, Mr. William Dunlap, the Park Theatre manager, accepted his new play to be included on the bill for that season. Julia or the Wonderer, a naughty comedy in five acts, was performed by the Park Theatre professional actors on February 7, 1806. John had written the play during seven late evenings as a satire on life in general. Although he named himself as playwright Eugenius, a gentleman of New York, most local people seemed to be aware of his identity, a young boy of 14 years. His use of profanity in the play, "damme" several times, and suggestive situations portrayed, shocked the critics who panned it, but delighted many in the audience. In the first act, Ranger (an immoral, corrupt young man) remarks to Frederick: "an obliging girl is worth all the wives in heaven." Julia the Wonderer was never performed again. John was appalled at the negative reaction of the press.

In preparation for his first year in college, John made a trip home to Boston not only to see his family, but also to be with Elizabeth before leaving for college. He knew from their correspondence that they had already arrived in Boston for the upcoming Theatre season. While David was busy several afternoons with Theatre arrangements, Elizabeth and John walked to the harbor and other familiar areas they had enjoyed in the past. They were older now and their relationship moved to a different dimension of time and experience. She accepted him as the wild and unpredictable fellow she had come to know and he, invariably attracted to pretty young or older ladies where ever he might be, found himself drawn always to Elizabeth, who was often in his thoughts. It has always been so that, what is most desirable, is that which cannot be had--- for whatever reason.

Chapter 7

At Union College
1806-1808

Mr. Payne wrote a letter to Dr. Aliphalet Knott, President of Union College, when he learned that Mr. John E. Seamen was providing John Howard with the opportunity to attend Union College.

Dear Dr. Knott:

Please allow me to introduce myself. I am the father of John Howard Payne, who will be a first year student this semester at Union College. John has been enrolled through the kindness of Mr. John E. Seaman, who is providing the financial wherewithal to make this available to him. I am headmaster of Berry Street Academy in Boston and with seven other children and my wife to support. Unfortunately, I would not be able to send him to Union College. Our family truly appreciates Mr. Seamons' kind generosity toward John. We all want to ensure that John Howard will use this fine opportunity to best advantage. Although he is the youngest of all my children, he is undoubtedly the one most capable of using college preparation to good advantage. John is precocious, keenly observant and learns quickly. He makes friends easily and is very creative. However, John has some traits which could be detrimental to his welfare. He is clever, but can be also recalcitrant, unpredictable and deceptive at times. For example, when he lived at home in Boston, on occasion after everyone in the household had retired, he would sneak out and often meet a friend. Together they would steal quietly down to the Boston Waterfront to observe the late night activity in the taverns and elsewhere. I did my best to control this mischief, but I wasn't always successful. Thank goodness that John and friend were not victimized by unscrupulous people in that environment. I'm hoping that by making you aware of this situation that you'll be able to deal with it effectively at Union College.

Sincerely,
William Payne
Head Master
Berry Street Academy

After reading Mr. Payne's letter, Dr. Knott, who wanted to maintain for Union College the interest and patronage of the very wealthy Mr. John E. Seaman, made an unorthodox arrangement which he felt certain would keep John in bed each night.

Of course John knew nothing of his father's letter. No matter. He was just pleased to be out of the counting house and away from Mr. Forbes. For him, college would be something to do while moving toward his passion to realize a career on the stage. However, he was disappointed that his patrons had chosen for him a college in Schenectady. Little did he know that Union College was an excellent choice. Founded in 1795, Union College was set on a magnificent campus complex and held a superb academic reputation. No matter. He would have preferred a more exciting environment with "city attraction" in the New York City area near the Park Theatre.

On his way home to Union College in Schenectady by riverboat, John made friends with a group of passengers including Charles

Brockdon Brown, a successful author of that period. John was younger than these acquaintances, all in their 20's and 30's who were traveling beyond his destination, but they all had common interests and social attitudes. John enjoyed this company so much that, instead of disembarking at his destination, he continued with the group to Montreal even though he had only $20 remaining pocket money from Mr. Seaman to cover travel expenses to college. When his money was spent, he borrowed funds from his new passenger friends to be able to return to Albany and college. This habit established early on to cover debt incurred from poor judgment was one problem which would continue to plague him throughout his life. Finally, he arrived at Union College two weeks after the fall term had begun. Dr. Knott, forewarned by William Payne, was prepared to handle John in an unorthodox arrangement.

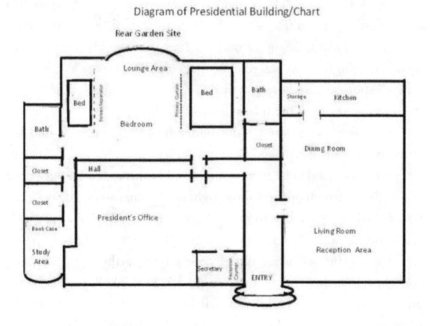

Dr. Knott's Suite

Fronting the heart of the main campus area, Dr. Knott's presidential quarters were an integral part of campus grounds and activity. In his large, well-equipped office, Dr. Knott maintained morning office hours from eight to twelve each morning except Sunday. Each of those afternoons were devoted to college operational affairs and funding development. Behind his office across the hall housed Dr. Knott's private quarters. The remaining half of the building was available for institutional use and social college activity offering a large dining area, a living room, and full-service kitchen. Three workers were employed for building operation. Miss Lydia Miller assisted Dr. Knott as his office secretary in the morning. Miss Maude Young tended to housecleaning services and Mrs. Stella Fry, the cook, had been serving Dr. Knott for nearly 30 years.

The private quarters used by Dr. Knott were located across the hall directly behind his office and contained one fourth of the floor space in the building. This provided ample room in his bedroom to accommodate, in addition, a small sitting area at the rear of the room looking out windows facing the backyard garden. Along the right length of the room, his bed was placed close to the main bathroom located next to his sleeping area. There was another small bathroom at the far left with a study alcove at the side in front of the bath.

Dr. Knott had ordered a dormitory bed to be brought into his bedroom for John and placed along the far left side wall of the bedroom outside the recessed cove next to the small bathroom. The only door exiting the bedroom opened at the right side of the room in front of Dr. Knott's bed, giving access to the hall and another door to his office. It was an unorthodox arrangement. Dr. Knott, a light sleeper, felt certain that he would be well aware of any door activity at the foot of his bed.

When John finally made his way back to the college two weeks later, he was advised of his unusual living quarters away from the other students. He would be sleeping in Dr. Knott's bedroom with the cove assigned as his study area. Although he was puzzled by the arrangement, his quarters were actually luxurious compared to the student dorm rooms normally assigned in Long Hall nearby. He soon

Morning 1808

became comfortable in his accommodations, especially since he was only required to sleep in Dr. Knott's bedroom, but not in the large bed with him.

John was doing well in his class work and making friends as usual. Dr. Knott's plan had succeeded in ending his night-time truancy. John's only annoyances were Dr. Knott's thunderous snoring and passing odiferous gas in bed.

John was even pleased with his class schedule. He was assigned morning classes each of the five days with two afternoon classes Tuesday and Thursday. He was free on Monday and Friday afternoons for study at the library or in his room alcove. He soon returned to his interest in publishing. Becoming involved before long in campus activity, he volunteered to be the editor of the college newspaper The Union News. After a few months had passed, he also initiated an additional little paper on November 10, 1806 which he named The Pastime. This biweekly publication was not entirely devoted to Theatre news like The Thespian Mirror published earlier in New York, while he was working at Forbes' Counting house. The Pastime focused upon writing, poetry, editorial comment and other literary themes. A number of selections were contributed by Union College students in each edition. The Pastime was popular and continued to appear for 21 issues ending in the spring of 1808. John made good use of his study cove in Dr. Knott's bedroom suite. College life at Union was enjoyable for John.

During Christmas break at home in Boston, John attended Federal Street Theatre where David and Elizabeth and the Ushers were acting. One evening he saw Thomas Dilden's Five Miles Off, a new play with Elizabeth as Laura Luckless and David as Edward. Another evening he enjoyed a performance of an old favorite Morton's Speed the Plough with Elizabeth as Miss Blandford and (this time) Luke Usher as Henry. John noticed that David Poe sometimes was assigned minor roles and even only walk-on parts.

John loved to be at the Theatre, if only in the audience, and he attended as often as he could. Elizabeth was always eager to see him backstage after the evening performances when he was there.

In anticipation of coming to Boston during Christmas break, John had found one day in a Schenectady gift shop a beautiful little musical jewelry box decorated on the top of the lid with a petite and pretty ballerina wearing a fluffy pink lace tutu, who twirled to the music box when it was activated from beneath. He gave her his gift after the Christmas Eve performance knowing he would be expected to be with the family on Christmas day. Elizabeth was delighted. It became her most prized possession for the rest of her life.

Unfortunately, John learned that he had to return to the college early, due to preparation of the upcoming editions of the two newspapers which would go to press on his last evening at the Theatre. Before leaving the next morning, he said goodbye to the Poe and Usher friends, telling them he looked forward to returning in the spring when the winter term ended.

Later when David discovered the Christmas gift from John (with misgivings) Elizabeth reminded him that John and she had been friends for years before David and she had even met.

Back at Union, there was remodeling preparation underway. The newly revised and upgraded Union News had become a popular addition to campus activity. The former newspaper quarters were enlarged with a new printing press and equipment and a well-appointed newspaper office fronting the hall. Dr. Knott, with board approval, had arranged funding for the project as a further educational offering for the many interested students now involved. He felt that his handling of the John Howard Payne situation had proven to be quite successful. John not only was a good student, but also had come to be a positive influence in campus activity. He was satisfied that he had accomplished what John's father could not. On Wednesday afternoon after the winter portion of the term had settled into routine, John gathered his class work notebook and realized he had forgotten to bring with him a report due that afternoon. Not wanting to be late to class, he left the newspaper office early to pick up the paper on his alcove desk as he made his way across campus to his classroom. Knowing Miss Miller would be gone for the day, John used his key to open the bedroom door. From his view at the front of Dr. Knott's bed, in front of him was an incredible surprise.

Morning 1808

Dr. Knott's bare skin and hairy legs were spread apart at the lower section of the bed. Maudie straddled the next body section in a bare bottom equestrian position, while the upper portion of Dr. Knott was enfolded in pillows under his head and Maudie's ample bosom on his face, muffling his hearing by his ecstatic loud screams of passion.

"Oooh, Maudie oh! Go faster, faster! Go faster! It's coming!" With his head at Maudie's breast and his loud response to the ride, Dr. Knott didn't hear John opening the door, but Maudie did. She turned her head and calmly gave John Howard a caustic smile and a sly wink. He quietly closed the door and hurried to class laughing all the way.

Friday afternoon couldn't come soon enough for John. He cleared his work at the newspaper office and hurried back to his quarters. Dr. Knott had a meeting in Albany which would culminate in a dinner and prayer. He informed John Howard at lunch that John would be dining alone that evening; however, he planned to return immediately to Union after the program.

Maudie was sitting on the bed when he came in. Supposedly she had just finished cleaning the room. He greeted her as he took off his coat and put his books away.,

"Thank you, Maudie, for not telling Dr. Knott that I saw you and him on the bed Wednesday afternoon. I knew I was safe when he was his usual self at dinner."

"No, I didn't tell."

"But Maudie I have thought of what was happening often since then. It was obvious from your glance to me at the door and your noticeable indifference that you weren't having a good time riding him."

"I never do, boy. It's just part of my job once or twice a week."

"How frustrating for you."

John Howard moved from his chair closer to the bed.

"Maudie, I know how to make it wonderful fun for both of us."

Maudie laughed, "For both of us? How amusing! John, you are hardly more than a little boy. What might you have heard about humping?"

John moved closer to her on the bed. "It's not what I have heard, Sassy, it's what I can do very well! And I'm almost 18 if that means anything. Are you afraid to let me show you? It would be our secret just between you and me."

Maudie was about to get up and leave, fearing Dr. Knott would find out somehow. But in spite of her inhibition, she felt a stirring within her and an urge which she did not want to resist as she watched his manner of undressing. John had had that effect on many young girls—and older women in the past which would continue. His sensual conquests through the years were endless (For example, after his death in fact), a romance with Mary Godwin Shelby was exposed to the public through letters found 80 years after the affair.)

Nevertheless on that Friday afternoon at Union College in Schenectady John with suggestive lewdness, slowly undressed Maudie in a foreplay she had never before experienced. From that afternoon on, they looked forward to Monday and Friday afternoons together.

The winter term at Union College concluded in early April with all departments reporting a good year. The College Board and Dr. Knott had anticipated commencement as a final achievement with many honors to bestow on the graduates. Although John was not a graduate that year, Dr. Knott decided to reward his academic accomplishment and his responsible demeanor throughout the winter term. For the next college year he would be given the opportunity to be housed in Long Hall as a regular student on campus. John was sure he would be able to handle that, also.

Chapter 8

Return to Boston
1806-1809

Luke and Nellie Usher were waiting for David and Elizabeth when they arrived in Boston after their summer theatre engagement in New York. It had been a happy summer, but both Elizabeth and David were looking forward to being in Boston. A number of improvements in the Federal Street Theatre had been made since Elizabeth had accompanied her mother's theatre troupe to Boston from London in 1795. Mr. Bullfinch, the current co-manager with Mr. Powell had remodeled the interior of the Theatre after the fire in 1798, adding many beautiful improvements. Boston now offered a much superior setting, drawing a cultured and more refined audience. No more catcalls or rough crowds throwing missiles at the actors on stage.

For opening night on October 13, 1806, the featured performance was Morton's comedy Speed the Plough with Elizabeth as Miss Blandford and David as Henry. It was a successful opening and the beginning of what would be a three year stay in Boston with occasional summer tours south. At the close of the evening, John's sister Lucy came backstage to deliver a congratulatory poem that John Payne had written in honor of their opening. John was on his way to Union College for the fall term.

Both couples, the Poes and the Ushers, seemed to enjoy some measure of success. Luke and Nellie had never commanded many starring roles, but were content to be very effective in playing important secondary roles often. Critics praised David's work at first, but soon panned his ability to animate his roles, sometimes even mispronouncing difficult proper names. Both David and Elizabeth were excellent dancers and the audiences enjoyed her singing, often clapping for an encore. Her command of Shakespearean language was outstanding; however, her petite, child-like figure was more effective in light comedy. In contrast, David's suave stage presence seemed to enhance the portrayal of Shakespearean male leads even though he had difficulty with the language.

In a few months Elizabeth knew that she and David were going to have a child in the winter. She hesitated telling David at first. Coming from a wealthy family, David was more sensitive to living at a near poverty level—the plight of actors in this era. He did not receive the news well. At first, he blamed Elizabeth for allowing herself to become pregnant. With little money, no suitable living quarters or available care for the baby while they were working, the problems would be overwhelming. However, he assured her that he would like to be a father in the future when their careers were established.

William Henry Leonard Poe was born on January 30, 1807. Even with his misgivings, David was proud of their handsome child. Years before when he left the study of law that his father had chosen for him, his parents were very disappointed. Becoming an actor and marrying a little English actress was the final transgression. They had disowned him.

David was certain that they would love the baby, who would be their first grandson. Perhaps the grandparents might even be moved to provide some financial assistance. In early spring, they traveled to Baltimore hoping to reconcile his relationship with General David Poe, his father. David counted on his mother's loving heart. They adored little William and even were pleased with Elizabeth's sweet personality.

While visiting there, Elizabeth met Maria Poe Clemm, David's seventeen year old cousin. They liked each other immediately. Maria was impressed with Elizabeth's beauty, grace and theatrical flair. They corresponded after that from time to time. Many years later, Elizabeth's son, Edgar Allan Poe would marry Maria's daughter Virginia Clemm on May 16, 1836 in Baltimore.

When the time came for David and Elizabeth to return to Boston for fall season preparation, the Poe grandparents loved baby William so much (as David had surmised), they asked to care for him while David and Elizabeth were in Boston during the fall season. However, William would stay with them permanently as it turned out.

Although the Boston years brought success in the Theatre, they were not happy years for the Poes. David had a fiery temper and was very sensitive to either criticism of him or of Elizabeth. Late in her pregnancy before the birth of William, she had been ridiculed by a local critic for her appearance as a boy, "Little Pickle" in Bickerstaff's play <u>The Spoiled Child</u>. The critic referred to her bulging figure as "suggestive of the hermaphroditical." Elizabeth had to enlist the help of Luke Usher to keep David away from attacking the critic physically.

As time passed, the Boston audiences became less friendly. This led to David becoming even more quarrelsome, demanding and finally, undependable. His name (and sometimes that of Elizabeth) was often not listed on theatrical announcements, indicating difficulties of a personal nature such as illness or absence. David often didn't appear on stage due to "indisposition," a polite term which indicated drunkenness.

Plagued by increased financial hardship due to his drinking and Elizabeth's desire to send small sums of money toward William's care, David often left to go to the Baltimore area in an attempt to borrow money from old friends or relatives. He had little success. At the end of their second winter season at Federal Street Theatre which closed on April 29, 1808, the Ushers had accepted a summer engagement at the Haymarket Theatre in Richmond. Elizabeth hoped to go with them, but David seemed to have lost interest in everything. He had continued to play some lead roles, but more often his periodic unaccounted-for absences away for a few days made it impossible to count on his presence on performance evenings.

One afternoon in early April, Elizabeth had a surprise visit form John Payne. He came to tell her that he was finished at Union college.

"The winter term has ended so soon? Don't you have final exams?"

John explained that the students with top grades were excused from exams and he was one of that group.

"I arrived home last evening and I'm not going back. As you know, my mother died last winter. Alone now, my father is having financial problems making ends meet at the academy. I told him I would stay in Boston this summer to help him with his problems to reorganize the school curriculum and student enrollment for the fall term. We had a long talk about my spending habits and my future—well, it was really an argument. But, I finally convinced him that I am determined to pursue a theater career, whatever else happens."

"Oh John, are you certain you have made the right decision not to finish college next fall and find a career making a lot of money? Just look at David and me. We would be happier, I think, if we had more money and fewer problems," said Elizabeth sadly.

"No more of this, little one! We're going to celebrate! First of all, we are finally together again and I have money to spend. We're going to have some fun like the old days in Boston—remember? Only we won't be watching other people enjoying themselves. It's our turn."

"John, where did you get money to waste?"

He corrected her. "Elizabeth, we will not waste it. Mr. Seaman was so proud that I had the best grade average in all of Union College this year, he gave me the rest of my unused yearly expense money as a gift."

"Ha!" said Elizabeth, "He won't feel so generous when he finds out you're not going back for your final year of commitment at Union college."

"Time enough to settle that. On my way up here to see you a fellow told me David had left Boston for a week on business—(a trip to find someone who will lend him some money, I think). But nevertheless, we can make our own plans."

"John, I have a show to do tonight, remember?"

Morning 1808

"Then, we'll leave after the show. A friend of mine has a place not too far from Boston—only he'll be out of town this week, fortunately for us," said John.

"John, you know I can't go. I have commitments here at the Theatre."

"The Ushers will take care of the situation for a few days," countered John.

"Are you forgetting that I'm married now? Our carefree days are over," protested Elizabeth.

"Elizabeth, I know this is not the time to bring up the past again, but if you had left David when I first begged you to leave with me several years ago, you never would have had to face dealing with David's bitterness now. Nothing has changed. He knew then that the critics were right and he was never going to be very successful on stage. So you deserve a little relief from the life you've been suffering with David's drinking, fiery temper and money-borrowing trips. Nobody will blame you—even if it is any of their business—which it isn't. Don't disappoint me. You know how much I have always loved you."

"We'll leave after the show. Roger, one of my close Union college friends, knows how much I was looking forward to being with you after the term ended. He was leaving this morning on a trip south with his family and gave me the key to a little apartment they own outside Boston on the seaside. Please don't waste this chance for us to be together at least for a weekend. I promise to have you back at the Theatre for Monday rehearsal."

John was waiting for her when she came off stage. He had hired a hackney which was waiting outside the Theatre stage door and they were on their way. The busy life of Boston soon seemed far away as they headed to the seaside community. While John paid the driver, Elizabeth admired their quaint little weekend retreat.

Chapter 9

A Very Memorable Weekend

What a lovely place to spend a weekend, Elizabeth mused to herself. John used Roger's key to open the door into a small but very comfortable living room with a fireplace surrounded by two inviting soft chairs and to the side, a small kitchen. The hall led to a well-appointed bedroom with a large bed decorated with many soft pillows and room for both of them, as John noted immediately with a discreet smile. Roger, as a treat for his friends, had left a tin of coffee and doughnuts to welcome them to their weekend get-away. And John had even brought with him a basket of provisions he had gathered to stock the kitchen for their needs. Everything was just right.

So many places to go; so many places to revisit. A trip to the Boston Harbor brought back many amusing incidents. The little storage building they had used at night, years before, was still there. Elizabeth blushed as John mused whether any other couple had used it for night visits. They finished their exploration, noticing an increase in the number of ships at dock. With picnic basket in hand, John led Elizabeth to their special hillside spot overlooking the harbor, where they enjoyed their picnic and dreamed of the future.

On Sunday afternoon, they enjoyed a gondola ride through the scenic waterways of the area. All the gondoliers provided a concert for the pleasure of their patrons. It was peaceful and relaxing—a perfect Sunday afternoon. As evening came, they dined at a popular Boston Tavern complete with more music and entertainment. Elizabeth wondered if they still sold Theatre tickets—

But night time found them as usual back at their little apartment. John built a fire and they spent hours each night enjoying their brief chance to be together.

On Sunday night as Elizabeth prepared for bed, she heard John laugh to himself. He told her that he treasured sleeping with her in his arms, while remembering his night time situation at college being awakened periodically by loud whistling snores and smelly flatulence emanating from far across the room. Of course, Elizabeth thought he was referring to other students in the dormitory. He told her that he would save that story for another day.

The weekend seemed to fly by so quickly, but they enjoyed every hour stolen from a life so different, left behind.

As John had promised, they returned to the Theatre on time for Monday rehearsal.

> Note: after her death, there was little left of Elizabeth's personal possessions to leave for her children. To little Edgar she bequeathed a sketch of Boston which she had made and named "Morning 1808." On the reverse side, she had written: "For my little son Edgar who should ever love Boston, the place of his "birth" and where his mother found her best and most sympathetic friends."

Chapter 10

The First American Hamlet

When the 1808 Boston season was coming to a close, Luke and Nellie Usher had invited Elizabeth and David to accompany them to Richmond for summer season at the Haymarket Theatre where they had been very successful during the previous summer. Elizabeth immediately responded to their invitation, hoping that possibly a few months away from the Boston area might lift David's spirits and pull him out of his physical depression and drinking habits. David did not share her enthusiasm. Over the years, David had developed a close friendship with Luke Usher. With this in mind, Elizabeth turned to Luke for support. After much discussion and soul-searching, Luke, with the help of Nellie and Elizabeth, convinced David that a summer in Richmond was what they all needed. As the pleasant southern summer evenings passed by, the Haymarket Theatre enjoyed the attendance of larger responsive audiences. Success has a positive effect in many ways. Even David, who had arrived in Richmond carrying a negative attitude, soon found himself lifted from his lethargy and self-defeating habits. The weekly performances included an assortment of old favorite plays and a few new comedies. Among those chosen were the following:

Cumberland's <u>The Sailor's Daughter</u>
Fielding's <u>Tom Thumb the Great</u>
Colman's <u>The Poor Gentleman</u>

Home's' <u>Douglas</u>
Murphy's <u>Three Weeks After Marriage</u>
Boaden's <u>The Maid of Bristol</u>

The time passed quickly and soon the summer season was coming to an end. The Ushers and Poes were gratified by both the Richmond public attendance and ticket sales. Nevertheless they were looking forward to returning to the more sophisticated setting of the Boston Theatre as fall approached.

However as summer passed, Elizabeth became aware of a situation she had not anticipated. She was pregnant again. Not only was her condition unexpected, she knew the child was not fathered by David. Remembering well his reaction to her pregnancy with Henry in 1807, she feared what was coming. David was so much better physically now than last winter. How could she avoid hurting him with the truth? Finally, Elizabeth confided in Nellie Usher who had been her mother figure since losing her own mother in the stage fire accident. Nellie was not surprised. She remembered Elizabeth's weekend with John after he left Union college at the end of the term in April. David had been gone on one of his absences during that week, she also remembered. Nellie immediately suggested naming her husband, David, as the father since by law he legally would be considered so. Elizabeth felt she couldn't accept that lie. So the secret remained.

The Boston season of 1808-1809 opened on September 26 with a varied program in place under the capable management of Snelling Powell. As introduced previously in 1807-1808, the current season would include not only offerings by the resident company which featured the Poes and Ushers, but also the use of new stars from time to time to add another dimension to the season repertoire. With the increased arrival of various stars from abroad, many successful managers now considered this novel option. In fact, both the Poes and the Ushers had become acquainted with Thomas Cooper and James Fennell while they were featured stars the winter of 1808.

Morning 1808

For example, when Cooper was in residence in January, Elizabeth played Ophelia to Cooper's <u>Hamlet</u> with David appearing as Laertes. With Cooper as <u>King Lear</u> in a later performance Elizabeth played Cordelia and David, the Duke of Albany. During Fennell's engagement, Elizabeth played both Ophelia and Jessica. Fortunately at that time, David was being cast in the more serious secondary roles to which he could relate.

However that was now in the past. James Fennell was again in residence when the 1808 season opened in September. Fennell's first appearance was as King Lear supported by Elizabeth as Cordelia and David as Edmund. David's improved health brought him more interesting and important roles. While Elizabeth played Arabella in Mrs. Cowley's play <u>More Ways Than One</u>, David was cast in the difficult "straight part" as Carlton in this social comedy. He also warranted the assignment as Ennui, a difficult role in Raynold's <u>The Dramatist</u>.

Elizabeth still had not told David that she was pregnant, still uneasy about how he might react this time. Finally, one evening as they were getting ready for bed, David asked, "Elizabeth, is there something you should share with me? Are we going to be parents again in a few months or so?"

"Oh, David, I know I should have told you I was pregnant before this," confessed Elizabeth, "but I--"

David interrupted her, "Please, dear, let me apologize. I know why you were afraid to tell me. I still regret my cruel reaction to you the night you told me you were pregnant with Henry. I'll never forgive myself for blaming you as if it were your fault. I would like to think I'm more mature now. When can we expect the baby to be born?"

As the months passed, David learned from a friend of a capable lady who needed to support herself and had worked as a nurse maid. She was again looking for a job when the family no longer needed her help. The Poes located an inexpensive small house not far from the Theatre, where Mrs. Berg could have a small bedroom/sitting room combination away from the Poes, but close to the awaited baby. Her wages would consist of room and board, in addition to a little pocket money as available. How they would be able to meet the monthly expenses was the question at hand. David and Elizabeth attempted to work constantly to be ready to support these planned obligations.

As John Payne had told Elizabeth when he came back to Boston after finishing his second year at Union College, he spent the summer helping his father put his affairs in order and reorganizing Berry Street Academy for more effective operation for the fall term of 1808. During his personal free time, John worked at journalism and at preparation of Theatre roles for his move to New York. In the fall when the Boston Theatre opened for the 1808-09 season, the Poes introduced John to Cooper, while he was there as an actor in residence. Thomas Cooper was an accomplished and well-known English actor, handsome, with dignity and nobility in his delivery and a great master with tragedy. After their introduction, John went to see him, hoping for some critical help with Theatre role interpretation. However, noting his obvious attraction for Elizabeth, Cooper refused to help him and tried to discourage John from pursuing a professional acting career. John never forgot this obvious slight.

On January 19, 1809, Elizabeth at age 25 years gave birth to a second son whom they named Edgar. After not being listed in the Theatre notices for the period of her recovery, The Boston Gazette welcomed Mrs. Poe back on February 9.

"We congratulate the frequenters of the Theatre on the recovery of Mrs. Poe from her recent confinement. This charming little actress will make her reappearance tomorrow evening as Rosamonda in the popular play of Abaellino the Great Bandit, a part peculiarly adapted to her figure and talents."

The article failed to note that Mr. Poe would be cast in the role of Contarino.

Despite Cooper's rebuff and attempts to discourage John in his pursuit of a stage career, John made good use of his personal time while in Boston helping his father. He worked on major roles in a number of popular plays of the era. Among those he prepared were:

Zaphna in <u>Mahomet</u>
Tancred in <u>Tancred and Sigismunda</u>
Rollo in <u>Pizarro</u>
Octavian in <u>The Mountaineers</u>
Romeo in <u>Romeo and Juliet</u>
Achmed in <u>Barbarosea</u>

John would let nothing stand in his way. He was going to have a stage career.

In January 1809, John returned to New York. He contacted Stephen Price, the co-manager with Thomas Cooper of the Park Theatre. The two well-known English actors had assumed management of this Theatre considered at that time to be the handsomest playhouse of the era with ornate furnishings decorated in blue and gold and with a greater seating capacity than Philadelphia, their competitor. The two co-managers had great plans for the future of the Park Theatre. Mr. Price was aware of John Howard Payne's earlier success as the editor and critic of a New York theatrical magazine and his work as a rising young playwright. With their blasé European background both Price and Cooper were amused by the reception of his first play, <u>Julia or The Wanderer</u> which—although it had delighted most of the audience, was condemned by the puritanical-influenced critics when it was presented at the Park Theatre for a single performance three years earlier.

With this in mind, and fearing that if they refused his request, John might seek a position with the Chestnut Street in Philadelphia, they engaged him immediately. At first, John seemed to be a fine addition and with his sweet voice, blue eyes and youthful appearance, he was soon given the sobriquet as "Master Payne" and well-received by the New York audiences. By the end of October, he was considered a full-fledged and respected Park Street stage performer appearing as young

Norval in <u>The Tragedy of Douglas</u> by John Home. But his association with Price and Cooper was weakened by an ugly disagreement over costumes and personal stage props. John decided to return to Boston.

John's popularity seemed to follow him. With Elizabeth as his Ophelia, he began his superb stage performance as America's First Hamlet. The <u>Boston Gazette</u> reported:

"The melancholy Dane has been portrayed before on the American stage, but never by an American. In Mrs. Poe, Payne found the perfect Ophelia."

A later review praised both John and Elizabeth for the credible and passionate stage portrayal of Romeo and Juliet.

Throughout the rest of the winter season, <u>Hamlet</u> was repeated by popular demand. John is acclaimed as the "First American Hamlet" with Elizabeth as Ophelia and David as Laertes. The season concluded with a double spectacle. The play <u>Pulaski</u> written by John, while attending his second year at Union College, was revised with lyrics added for Elizabeth's performing talents. In its new format, the play was renamed <u>Lodoiska or the Captive Princess</u>.

Unfortunately with the presence of Thomas Cooper, and soon after John's return, David was forced to accept minor roles again. Not only did this cause his resentment, he became acutely aware of both Cooper's and John's personal attentions to Elizabeth.

With both Elizabeth and David on stage steadily, their finances were improving—even Mrs. Berg was allotted a bit more pocket money. Knowing of their added expenses, Mr. Powell on occasion announced the performance that evening as a "benefit night" for the

Morning 1808

Poes. John also tried to help, giving them a portion of his assigned "benefit nights" also. It was difficult for David to accept John's generosity graciously.

Little Edgar had become a favorite of the theatre crew—both on stage and backstage. Shortly after his birth, the manager of the stage properties found, in a far corner of the basement storage area, a long-unused baby carriage. The stage hands scrubbed it thoroughly and with a fresh coat of paint and four new wheels, presented it as a gift to a very appreciative mother and father. Weather permitting, Mrs. Berg took Edgar on a daily walk, sometimes stopping at the theatre for a few minutes when rehearsals were underway. Edgar was a handsome, chubby little fellow with his mother's dark expressive eyes and blond baby soft curly hair. As young as he was, he responded to the attention of his stage family with happy gurgles and baby cooing sounds.

As it would turn out, the three year engagement in Boston would conclude the Theatre experience for the Ushers. Mrs. Elizabeth Arnold (Beth to her family and friends) and Mrs. Nellie Snowdon had been friends since appearing on the London Stage at the Theatre Royal in Covent Gardens in the late 1780's after Nellie's husband died. She followed "Beth" Arnold and little Betty to Boston. Their friendship had continued through the years working in Theatre and Nellie eventually marrying Luke Usher. Elizabeth had always been grateful for their kindness to her after her mother's accident.

Luke's background was very different from that of his wife, Nellie. He had been born and reared on a farm outside a small town (Leesburg) in Northwestern Virginia on the banks of the Potomac River. Luke, as a teen, decided being a farmer wasn't very exciting. Thus he soon met Nellie. However, he never lost contact with his family in Leesburg, returning some years in the summer season to the beautiful farm bordering the Potomac River.

After his father's death, Luke's older brother, Homer, who never had married, stayed on the farm. During their last Christmas visit the year before (1808), Homer who was older than Luke had asked Luke and Nellie to come back to help him run the farm which would become Luke's farm eventually. They had been thinking of retirement for some time and decided this was the perfect opportunity. Homer would have the help he needed and they would have a comfortable place of their own.

Elizabeth and David were sorry to see them leave, but understood their situation. Besides, the Ushers had invited them to come for a visit often and bring Edgar!

The Poes had not attempted to find a summer Theatre engagement when the season ended. After Edgar was born in January, David, never satisfied with their meager finances, better than in the past, but not up to David's tastes, had traveled to Baltimore again as in the past, to borrow money from friends and relatives. He found little success embittered by their refusals. Only his cousin, Maria Poe, was receptive to him. She had no money to lend but invited David, Elizabeth and Edgar to come to Baltimore for a visit when the season ended. Away from his Boston problems seemed to calm David somewhat from his suppressed anger and jealousy of his loss of leading star roles on stage and John Payne's obvious personal interest in Elizabeth. Although Maria was pleased by their visit and a very hospitable hostess, David's parents were embarrassed by David's repeated quest for loans from family members and their welcome was strained at times during the summer.

Chapter 11

Summer in Baltimore 1809

Without the responsibility of the usual seasonal summer engagement, David, Elizabeth and six-month-old Edgar enjoyed a relaxing visit to be with the Poe relatives in Baltimore. Throughout the past winter, she and Mrs. Berg, who also had accompanied the family to Baltimore, had made little gifts to take each family member with several special toy rattles they had made for both Henry and his little brother Edgar. Elizabeth hoped Henry wouldn't forget the three of them during the long periods of time that they would be away from Baltimore, which had become Henry's home now. Maria Poe Clem was delighted with Edgar who looked so much like his mother, and enjoyed rocking him to sleep whenever she could. Many years later, as his mother-in-law, she would remember that visit, rocking "Eddie," her later grown-up nickname for him.

Of course, without their usual summer engagement, lack of money was a problem as always. David's major purpose for the trip was obvious. However his continuous attempts to borrow money from relatives and old friends embarrassed his father. Their only respite had been living (and boarding) with family during the summer with few expenses otherwise.

Even though David didn't know, Elizabeth and John corresponded regularly and John knew they were in Baltimore. A letter arrived telling Elizabeth that he had secured a position for them in the fall season in

New York at the Park Theatre. Elizabeth was ecstatic. To be in New York at the very sophisticated Park Theatre and to act again with the handsome English actor, Thomas Cooper, was wonderful news—but she also realized that somehow, she would have to convince David to accept graciously the secondary roles that he might be offered. John explained that Steven Price, the manager who had engaged Thomas Cooper again while in London, knew that Elizabeth would be a compatible female lead to complement him on stage. In the letter, John said that he would be late arriving since he had family commitments in Boston to complete. He also told her that his financial situation was now stable and when the winter season ended, it would be time for them to leave together, a plan postponed for too long. Of course, Elizabeth didn't share all the contents of his letter with David.

Finally Elizabeth had achieved her New York break. In September, they said goodbye to the family in Baltimore and moved to be a part of a more sophisticated New York setting. With Steven Price as manager and the arrival of visiting London actors successful abroad, Theatre audiences developed into more gentile, mature, and even liberal viewers, more like those in attendance abroad. Even in Boston, the long shadow of Puritanism had become less of a controlling factor in themes. New York audiences even seemed less critical of moral depiction as actors assumed the stage role in the play. If the play was appropriately performed and well-received on any given evening, well-wishers or Theatre fans might be waiting at the stage door to compliment the actors after the show. Occasionally an actor might even be recognized by these stage door visitors somewhere on the city streets or possibly at market.

As the Park Street season progressed, Elizabeth played opposite Thomas Cooper in a variety of popular, or even new plays Cooper had used successfully with audiences at Covent Gardens. Among those used, the following selections seemed to be American audience favorites:

> Cooper as Captain with Elizabeth as Priscilla Tomboy
> in M. G. Lewis' <u>The Castle Spectre</u>
> Cooper as <u>Hamlet</u> to Elizabeth's Ophelia

Morning 1808

O'Keeffe's <u>Modern Antiques</u>
Colman's <u>We Fly By Night</u>
Charles Kemble's <u>Bridget of Blunders</u>
Robert Jephson's <u>Two Strings to Your Bow</u>
Garrich's <u>The Suspicious Husband</u>

Their line interpretation enhanced that of the other, and they worked well together. The audience loved them. However, David was cast in bit parts and sometimes not at all. He again is criticized severely and retaliated (as he had in the past) with physical attacks on the critics—if he could find them. Heavy drinking resulted in absence on performance night. Soon his periodic heavy coughing spells were also unpredictable.

Elizabeth appeared often four evenings each week with Thomas Cooper, but it would soon be the time he was scheduled to return home. While Elizabeth was finally gaining success on the stage, her personal life was falling apart. David seemed defeated through a sense of failure. They quarreled often due to his feelings of futility and jealousy concerning her theatre associations with John and others with whom she worked. He now started again leaving for days at a time without a reason. She never knew where he went or when he might return.

One night in early February Elizabeth was confronted with the most frightening ordeal of her entire life. If ever she needed David, it was then—but he was not there. After the evening performance was over, she was delayed with making some repairs of ripped clothing needed for the next scheduled performance. Returning to her dressing room before leaving, she became aware of a man hiding at the far side of the room in the shadows.

Trying to assuage her fears, she asked him in a quavering, but stern, voice how he had been able to get through the locked dressing room door and why he had broken in. When he stepped out of the dark corner, she recognized him as one of the occasional stage door visitors and she remembered something else.

"I believe I've seen you sometimes when Edgar and I were in the park on Sunday afternoon."

After a long silence he answered, "Yeah, I've been watching you for quite awhile." He was a stalker! "It wasn't hard to force your dressing room window open."

With anxiety, she rushed back toward the door leading to the hall, but he had anticipated her move. He grabbed her long hair as she turned to free herself from his grasp. She shivered with fear when she heard his mean, sinister growl, but hot anger overcame her fear, knowing what he had in mind. He roared in pain as she used her long pointed nails to scratch his face from his forehead to his throat. He was right behind her as she bolted to the door. As she stumbled, he hit her head with the heavy tool he had used to force open the window. She dropped to the floor as she blacked out.

Slowly regaining consciousness, she tried to scream from excruciating pain, but he had stuffed a towel in her mouth. He was lying on top of her small body, heaving and gasping . When she tried to push him away, she couldn't move her arms. He had bound her wrists to the heavy iron heating stove over her head. She was helpless. She dimly was aware of her rapist opening the dressing room door to leave while fastening his pants. She hoped that, in the darkness backstage, he would fall over the stacked storage equipment by the door and alert the house cleaning crew who had arrived.

He laughed at her agony and defeat. "That's what you get for thinking you're so fancy!"

At the open door of her dressing room, he stopped short, hearing noisy activity in the Theatre area. The cleaning crew was sweeping out the seating area and preparing for the upcoming week. Hurrying into the hall in the darkness of the unfamiliar back stage area, as Elizabeth had hoped, he had knocked over some stacked storage equipment by the door.

"Who's up there? What are you doing?" "Don't try to get away. Come down here now."

"What are you trying to steal?"

All talking at once, the crew came running with lamps to back stage to find the intruder. But the intruder had finally stumbled through the door and disappeared behind the Theatre.

Morning 1808

The two women workers, noticing that Elizabeth's door was open, were aghast when they reached her. Her wrists were bleeding; her dress was on her face. Her clothes were torn and bloody. She was bruised with dirty handprints. At the door they tripped over her pantalets, lying beside her in shreds.

When the men were made aware of Elizabeth's condition, they ran out backstage to find the rapist.

"We'll catch that bastard!"

"Yeah—we'll get him and then kill him!"

But the intruder was gone—and never seen again.

The women did what they could for Elizabeth while the men unlocked the barn behind the Theatre. They took the horse and wagon up to the stage door in the rear, one of the crew was there carrying Elizabeth, crying softly to herself, who had been wrapped in a blanket by the two women.

Elizabeth was comforted to know that Mrs. Berg was at home with Edgar. She would need the weekend to regain her strength to be back for Monday rehearsal, and she was also grateful that she could always count on Mrs. Berg, who had lived through a long life of bad experiences. More was yet to come.

Chapter 12

Alone

As John had promised in his letter, he returned to the Park Theatre for a series of performances in March 1810 because he wanted to act with Elizabeth. Mr. Price agreed to his return, hoping for a more positive association with John Howard Payne whose current acclaim would be an asset to the Park.

He and Elizabeth were finally together again. The New York critics praised their incomparable rapport.

> "Mrs. Poe shared in the Ovations that greeted 'Master Payne's return to the Park Theatre. She was Cora, the priestess of the Sun. She was Payne's Ophelia; she was his impassioned Juliet. She glowed in the rapturous aura of the prodigy John Howard Payne."
>
> Critics of the <u>Broadway Journal</u>

However, in time John was soon quarreling with the English actors, who were jealous of his success and with Steven Price who resented John's request for special treatment after becoming a "star." Before he left, he asked Elizabeth to meet him in Richmond for the summer season.

Elizabeth, four months pregnant, and David were not rehired at the Park, so they, with Edgar and Mrs. Berg, gathered their few worldly belongings and joined Mr. Placide's Virginia Company in Richmond for the summer season. John wasn't there waiting to join them immediately, as he had been requested by his family to appear in a Washington engagement which would delay his plans to arrive in Richmond. For John, Elizabeth had learned, anything could be put on hold if expedient—

Elizabeth had become quite concerned about David. She thought often of the person he was in 1804, confident in his pursuit of an acting career. Born into a prosperous family with an admirable background, David had a life of comfort and respect, lacking nothing that money could buy. General Poe, his father, had known his son had the ability to pursue a successful law career. However, David refused his father's offer, never imagining what he would come to endure through his decision to pursue an acting career. He never expected the verbal abuse of the critics, the financial insecurity, the bitterness from ridicule and the unstable lifestyle. His naive pursuit of a stage career had lead to his loss of integrity and personal downfall. Elizabeth understood the pain of his defeat. She had learned from childhood to accept "living on the edge" as a normal existence, hoping always for success. She could endure any possible drawback that might appear. Only a few realized their dreams.

In addition to his problems, David had discovered John's letters where Elizabeth had concealed them. They confirmed the whispers he had heard. He was not Edgar's father—Edgar was John's son. And now Elizabeth was pregnant from the rape.

In July 1810, David disappeared. In vain, Elizabeth waited for his return. She wrote to the Ushers, remembering David's friendship with Luke. She wrote to the family in Baltimore. Where he had gone remained a mystery. One report came to her of his death in a saloon fight in Boston. Another source claimed that he was alive in 1810 and went abroad with a Philadelphia acting troupe.

The 1810 summer season at Richmond Theatre turned out to be a smashing success. When Elizabeth arrived, Mr. Placide introduced her to a new foreign star, George Frederick Cooke, who had been recruited by Thomas Cooper to visit the United States. Upon meeting him, Mr.

Placide had engaged the new actor also for the summer season. Even though Thomas Cooper warned Mr. Placide that, although Cooke had was an outstanding actor, he had a drinking problem, which caused many Theatre managers to consider as a negative to his performance. Mr. Placide's decision to take a chance on Cooke was providential.

The summer passed quickly with a large, responsive audience at all performances. Among the most applauded for Elizabeth were:

    Angela in <u>The Castle Spectre</u>
    Florence in Tobin's <u>The curfew</u>
    Emma in Colman's <u>We Fly By Night</u>
    Rosa in Reynold's <u>The Caravan</u>

She sang a number of familiar songs during the months which included one of her mother's favorites from their early years in Boston "Nobody Coming to Marry Me" included in a long series of songs by the company.

Mr. Placide was pleased with Elizabeth's work and invited her to stay on for the upcoming fall season even though she would be off stage for confinement during the baby's birth period. He knew she was popular with the community.

It was necessary for Mr. Placide to delay the opening of the winter 1810 season for two unforeseen drawbacks. A severe outbreak of yellow fever in Charleston had spread throughout the south. It was a constant problem which threatened every summer. An even greater drawback resulted from candles overturned during late summer Theatre repairs. Fortunately the Theatre wasn't completely destroyed. The opening night was moved to October.

While working with Elizabeth, Mrs. Berg had unwittingly developed a small business for herself. Before coming to help Elizabeth, Mrs. Berg had been a seamstress in her early years. Now she made baby clothes for the children and repairs or alterations for Elizabeth and herself, when needed. From Mrs. Phillips millinery shop customers, she began to take order requests for copies of items she had made for the children. Since Elizabeth was so near time for the baby, under Mrs. Berg's tutelage, she learned to help Mrs. Berg with the clothing orders she had gathered. Elizabeth was going to be off stage for awhile and the money they earned together provided a source of income.

On November 13, 1810, the baby Rosalie was born late at night. Even though the child's conception had been an unforeseen act of violence, ugly and unwarranted for Elizabeth, Rosalie was a darling, sweet-natured little soul. She looked like her mother with a cute little smile, pretty blue eyes and soft, blond curly hair. She immediately charmed everyone who came to see her. Sometimes nature's precious gifts come in a strange disguise.

After Rosalie was born, Elizabeth had hoped to return to the stage for the remainder of the winter season, but that was not to be. Elizabeth's health was slow to return. She was weak and bedfast and unable to regain her strength as quickly as she had hoped.

The winter season ended early in April 1811. Mr. Placide needed time to complete some temporary repair to the Richmond Theatre which had hastily been done after the fire had delayed the winter season opening until October. Mr. Placide's restoration was completed successfully and all was read by late summer.

The 1811 fall season at the Richmond Theatre opened on August 16. Elizabeth was again on stage through September and October playing a number of current favorites. Among them were:

> Bridget in Kemble's Budget of Blunders
> Emily in Dr. Door's The Battle of Eutaw
> Lydia in T.C. Cross' Love Laughs at Locksmiths with
> various popular vocal selections included.

But Elizabeth's health was deteriorating. Childbearing, the stress of a hard life, constant worry and childcare had taken its toll of her strength. Also, she had become less active with the arrival of Mrs. Beaumont, a star from Covent Gardens, who was more effective playing in Shakespearean roles. Elizabeth now had consumption, but was forced to sing and dance and to smile while inside her spirit was broken. Her last stage appearance came late in October.

Chapter 13

Finale

Unable now to act, due to prolonged coughing spells, or to even go to the Theatre, Elizabeth lived with Mrs. Berg and her children in the upstairs rooms at Mrs. Phillip's boarding house next to the Indian Queen Tavern. The tavern was a popular meeting place for actors, their friends and local people who enjoyed theatre. Mrs. Phillips' millinery shop customers also had befriended Elizabeth earlier, when she had arrived at the Theatre on stage the year before. These ladies represented the typical kindhearted, helpful nature of southern people. Now they visited her sick room to supply food and sympathy as her illness became much worse. At the Theatre, many benefits were given for her at this time also. The last of these benefits was presented on November 29, 1811. Elizabeth died on Sunday morning, December 8, 1811 "ending a career, though honorable, full of labor, anxiety and poverty." Entry from The Richmond News

The children were taken the next day by two prominent Richmond families, Edgar to live with the John Allans and Rosalie, to live with the William Mackenzies. Mrs. Berg also accompanied Rosalie to her new family home. Mr. Mackenzie had employed Mrs. Berg to serve as a part of their household staff caring for their children and Rosalie.

All that Elizabeth had to give as a material legacy to her children was an empty jewel box to Rosalie and to Edgar, a miniature of herself and sketch of Boston which she had drawn in happier days. There was also a mysterious packet of letters which Mr. Allan kept for Edgar. In later years, Edgar willed that this packet should be burned at his death. This strange request was carried out by Mrs. Clemm, his aunt and mother-in-law, as he had specified. Whatever information was contained therein was carefully guarded by Edgar.

For Elizabeth, Still Close to Greatness

A controversy arose regarding an appropriate place to bury the pathetic little actress, Elizabeth Poe. Some Richmond people objected to her burial with respectable people. However, through the defense of Mr. and Mrs. Allan on Tuesday, December 10, 1811, she was laid to rest at St. John's Episcopal Church Cemetery, buried in a place apart, in an unmarked grave close to the eastern wall.

Today many tourists visit St. John's Episcopal Church in Richmond. But their reason may not be to visit the grave of the little actress, Elizabeth Arnold Hopkins Poe. The event which has given St. John's historical significance is the occasion at which Patrick Henry delivered his famous speech before the House of Burgesses in 1775. Visitors may stand on the very spot where he declared, "Give me liberty or give me death!" But few visit Elizabeth Arnold lying in a grave apart, close to the eastern wall. She remains close to greatness, but not a part of it.

Many years later, a small grave stone was placed at her gravesite by important local people, part of a group which had long appreciated her legacy through her son Edgar.

Chapter 14

John Howard in Washington and Abroad

John never did return to Richmond from the Washington engagement with his family. When James Madison was elected the 4th President of the United States in March 1809, the Payne family was often included in high society affairs in the Capitol. The first Lady, Dolley Madison, a beautiful widow, whose first husband had died with yellow fever earlier, was now a perfect white House hostess. Born Dorothea Payne, she was an outgoing member of the very large and prominent Payne clan. Her father and John's father were cousins. Any or all Payne relatives were often invited to the many social levees, along with members of Congress, foreign visitors, and other important guests. The President himself presided at most of these gathering or soirées, if held in the evening. Elegantly attired Ladies and Gentlemen were served refreshments with appropriate music as a background for personal conversation. If Payne cousins had traveled a distance to attend, they were invited to remain for a period of time, often a week or two.

At first, John felt very comfortable as part of the ongoing Washington social whirl, but, in time, became even weary of the opulent lifestyle.

When John learned of Elizabeth's death in Richmond in December of 1811 and his father's death in March of the following year 1812, he regretted his many broken promises. He was bored and looked for another project to pursue. Soon another opportunity appeared.

He was approached by some Baltimore friends one afternoon at a White House reception to join a group with government backing to visit Europe. He quickly agreed to go with them. The American stage had lost its appeal. As it turned out, he stayed abroad for many years. Over the years, he was involved in a number of fortuitous happenings—and also some others.

1. He engaged in three or four love affairs, one with a married lady (her husband traveled frequently in his profession). All ended amicably.
2. He re-established his friendship with Henry Brevoort, an old friend from early Union College years.
3. When the war was over, he moved to Paris at the invitation to join Washington Irving with translating French plays to sell to English stage managers for use on the London stage. It was a lucrative project until copyright problems arose. Irving advised him to return to America, but John's refusal to go back with him resulted in a short prison term for John (who was deemed the primary translator.)
4. While in prison, John wrote his only famous, long standing composition, the song "Home Sweet Home" which he had written as a part of the play Clari or A Promise of Marriage.
5. His last position was awarded to him by President Tyler who appointed him government consul diplomatic representative in Tunis in February 11, 1843. He served in this capacity as a diplomatic representative until his death on April 9, 1852. He was finally interred in Washington's Oak Hill Cemetery after an appropriate public procession through the city streets and a ceremony conducted by the President of the United States, Chester A. Arthur, who was also a graduate of Union College, where John Howard Payne's name was remembered with high regard as part of Union College tradition.

Morning 1808

Rationale

From all that has been written over the years about Edgar, the question of Edgar Allan Poe's paternity has never been authentically established. Usually sources either discreetly treat the issue or, in many instances, ignore it completely. Why?

From David Poe's first appearance on stage in 1804, although he was tall and handsome, his lack of acting skills was constantly maligned by the critics. Before long he resorted to negative behavior as he was given only minor roles-or none at all. By 1807, his heavy drinking, indisposition on stage and little income caused his frequent trips away in attempts to borrow money from his well-to-do family and friends. These trips away—either through disappointment in unsuccessful loans (or repayment) or drunken disability resulted in longer absences more often. David finally disappeared without returning in July 1810.

John Payne flitted in and out of Elizabeth's life from their first meeting backstage in Boston 1795, until his last stage appearance with her in 1810. He was with her when he finished the 1808 term at Union College and returned home to Boston, where Elizabeth was on stage during the conclusion of the winter season in early spring 1808. There is much evidence from many sources that he was indeed the father of Edgar.

The well-known historian of this era, Arthur Hobson Quinn in his History of the American Drama, has called attention to the striking resemblance between Poe and Payne:

. . . He (Payne) was a precocious child and, like Edgar Poe, seems to have been of a highly wrought nature, and to have had a fondness and a fitness for the companionship of his elders. Like Poe, too, he was a leader in the athletic sports of his school, and one of his schoolmates tells how as a boy of 12 he was the captain of the "Boston Federal Band," a completely equipped military company. . . . (pg. 163)

They shared many physical traits as well. A description of Payne given by Henry P. Hedges refers to his "fair and florid countenance, eyes large and blue and forehead high and white," handsome with dark hair and slight stature. Except for the eye color, the description applied as well to Edgar.

The resemblance between Edgar and his older brother Henry was slight. According to Hervey Allen, Henry was a willowy youth, somewhat taller than his younger brother. Both had their mother's deep, dark eyes.

Payne and Poe also shared common salient character traits and aptitude for work. Besides his stage career, John Howard Payne was a creative person, during his lifetime writing plays, essays, and poetry. It was his work as a journalist and literary critic which first brought him public recognition. All of these interests are reflected (and intensified in importance) in the career of Edgar Allan Poe.

Henry had been cared for by his father's parents in Baltimore since infancy, but when Elizabeth Poe died on December 8, 1811, none of the Poe family came forth to take charge of the two small orphans, Edgar and Rosalie. With the grudging consent of her husband, John Allan, Frances Allan carried Edgar home and into her heart; Rosalie was taken into the William Mackenzie family. Why were these children exempt from the concern felt for Henry four years earlier? Letters written to the Allans and Mackenzies from Poe family members do not question custody of the children. They had good reason to reject kinship with the orphans.

Each of the persons, through whose hands the packet of letters that Edgar had inherited from his mother, had different reason for keeping their contents secret. However, in each instance, the reasons seem to hinge upon Edgar's illegitimacy rather than Rosalie's alone.

John Allan, who first held the letters, was a vindictive man whose personality reflected "a glitter of steel and an affected piety." His mental abuse of Edgar throughout his lifetime seemed to stem from his jealousy of the deep love his wife felt for the boy, her only child. During his first marriage, while Edgar was growing up, John Allan engaged in numerous extra-marital affairs and produced at least two or three illegitimate children, unknown to his wife. If the letters had proven only Rosalie's birthright, Allan probably would not have valued their contents so dearly since her fate was of no concern to him. But if the correspondence related to Edgar's parentage, this would provide leverage for him in dealing with the boy he so resented and feared.

Morning 1808

In his lifetime, Edgar was fiercely protective of his mother and sister, attempting to shield them from moral criticism of any kind. At various times, he attempted to alter the death dates of his parents to occurring a few weeks apart. He also claimed in one instance that Rosalie was older than he. The great pride in his mother that he carried throughout his life is reflected in a tribute to her which appeared in an article in 1845:

> The writer of this article is himself the son of an actress—has invariably made it his boast--and no earl was ever prouder of his earldom than he of his descent from a woman who, although well born, hesitated not to consecrate to the drama her brief career of genius and of beauty. (Broadway Journal, II [July 19, 1845], 29.)

His reasons for shielding the letters from public disclosure are clear.

Maria Clemm, who became his mother-figure and later his mother-in-law, had a genuine affection for "Eddy," as she called him. The letters caused her undue perturbation and she sometimes referred to their "great mystery." Mary Devereaux also reported that Mrs. Clemm had hinted in her presence of "some family mystery, of some disgrace." (From Hervey Allen in Israfel) Mrs. Clemm dutifully carried out Eddie's wishes when she burned the letters at his death.

That she would have done so to protect Rosalie hardly seems likely. Mrs. Clemm and Rosalie disliked each other and engaged in a vicious legal battle after Edgar's death over his few personal possessions and posthumous earnings. Any evidence to have discredited Rosalie as his rightful heir would have been to Mrs. Clemm's advantage. For Mrs. Clemm, who was nearly destitute, this financial help was desperately important. Since she chose not to pursue vengeance on Rosalie, which the letters would surely have provided, we must only assume the information was damaging to Edgar also.

But the letters are gone and John Howard Payne's fame rests upon his writing of the well-known song "Home Sweet Home". His life was filled with love affairs. W. T. Hanson wrote:

Evidence . . . tends to show that Payne was not unlike the proverbial sailor, with his 'girl in every port'. Certain it is that the number of the opposite sex with whom at various times, he believed himself desperately in love could not be counted on the fingers of both hands.

Overmyer added that "he was constantly in the state of being 'almost in love' during his lifetime, but never completing the final commitment."

If David had written some of the letters Elizabeth cherished, one can imagine the bitter recriminations and his agonized farewell. Perhaps letters from Payne would have offered an apology for not supplying legal, moral or financial support: she was married, he had commitments and, at that time, no money. Familiar excuses. Maybe Payne was remembering her when he wrote some of the songs given in another section of this book. In the play <u>Woman's Revenge</u> from which it is taken, the parting line Payne gave to the heroine concluded: "The right revenge is woman's – to forgive."

Source References

Allen, Hervey. Israfel. New York: Farrar & Rinehart, Inc., 1934.
Bittner, William. Poe. London: Elek Books, 1962.
Campbell, Killis. "Some Unpublished Documents Relating to Poe's Early Years." Sewance Review, 20 (1912), 201-212.
Gill, William F. The Life of Edgar Allan Poe. New York, 1877.
Hanson, W. T. Early Life of John Howard Payne. Boston, 1913.
Harrison, Gabriel. Life and Writings of John Howard Payne. New York, 1885.
Hislop, Cadman, and W. R. Richardson, eds. The Last Duel in Spain and Other Plays. Vol. VI of America's Lost Plays. Ed. Barrett H. Clark. Princeton: Princeton Univ. Press, 1940.
Ketcham, Ralph. James Madison. University of Virginia Press. 1990.
Overmyer, Grace. America's First Hamlet. New York: University Press, 1957.
Payne, John Howard. "Random Scraps and Recollections from the Notebook of a Wanderer." The Ladies Companion, August, 1837.
Phillips, Mary E. Edgar Allan Poe, the Man. 2 Vols. Philadelphia, 1926.
Pullen, John J. "Artemus Ward and the Moral Majority." The Plain Dealer, Sunday Ed. 21 Feb. 1982, Magazine, pp. 23-26.
Quinn, Arthur Hobson. Edgar Allan Poe: A Critical Biography. New York: Appleton-Century-Crofts, Inc., 1941.
A History of the American Drama: from the Beginning to the Civil War. 2nd ed. New York: Appleton-Century-Crofts, Inc., 1943.

Wilson, Garff B. Three Hundred Years of American Drama and Theatre. Prentice-Hall, Inc., Englewood Cliffs, N. J. 1973.

Winwar, Frances. The Haunted Palace: A Life of Edgar Allan Poe. New York: Harper, 1959.

Selection of Poems by John Howard Payne

"Flattery"

>Lines addressed to a lady who told the author she feared that the attention of the world would spoil him, and unfit him for anything serious. Written in 1806

Oh, Lady! Had'st thou ever seen
The tear unbidden fill my eye,
Or mark'd me in the sportive scene,
To half suppress the rising sigh,--

Thou wouldst not think that Pleasure's
Had blinded and subdued my heart.
Or planted deep was, rankling there
The person of her glittering dirt!—

True, fortune on my boyhood smiled
And much of flattery I have known,
Yet Sorrow claims me as her child,
And early mark'd me for her own.

The' joy has burst its prison chains,
And rapture started from its sleep,
They left me with severer pains,
They taught me better how to weep!

Few are the hours which beam like those
That I have sweetly spent with you,
Which, brilliant 'mid a cloud of woes,
In memory still their charms renew!

On the death of a lady Friend

Death with reluctant steps, half lingering, kiss,
And, armed with terror, pitying, shakes his spear!
He strikes, and as the lovely victim dies,
Relenting, mourns her with a silent tear!

The Coquette

Of, tell me, sweet girl, ere we part,
If your recent reproofs were sincere,
If that anger arose from the heart,
Which glowed in those glances severe..

Did you mean, love, when lately we met,
In earnest to frown thus and fly me?
Or, acting for once the coquette,
Did you counterfeit rage but to try me?

Come! Kiss and make up ere we part,
And, dearest, I'll strive to amend!
For, depriv'd of my home in your heart,
Where again shall I find such a friend?

Canzonet

Thou, oh, thou hast lov'd me, - dearest!
When none other cared for me,
When my fortune seem'd severest,
Kindest was the smile from thee!

Yes, --ay, yes! The lorn and lonely
Hollow hearts of worldlings sheen.
Theirs are flowers of day, which only
Open when they see the sun.

But while theirs were all reposing
In the absence of the light,
Like the cereus, thine, unclosing,
Gave its sweetness to the night.

The Loss of Those We Love

The pang, of all severest,
Is the deep, withering one, that's borne
In being torn
From those we love the dearest.

Some griefs bear consolation!
There's none for this, no, none! It breaks
The heart, and makes
The world a desolation!

A Girl's Message to Her Lover

I

Tell him, though fortune dooms that we must part,
I cannot make his image leave my heart;
Tell him that they may keep me from him, -- yet
He's with me still, as though we hourly met.

II

Wealth and Glories, tell him, all are dim
To the sweet sunshine of one thought of him,--
And feelings, deeper than the tongue can tell,
Have grown even deeper since I sigh'd Farewell!

The Girl of My Heart

There's nothing, there's nothing so lovely that lives
    As thou art, dear!
There's nothing, there's nothing that pleasure gives,
    And thou art near!

When thou art away the world's brightest charms
    Look – oh, how drear!
But a magic spell its form disarms
    When thou art near!

When thou art away, even summer's beams
    All cold appear!
But the coldest winter a summer seems
    Beside thee, dear!

Silently

    Silently, silently
Manage this affair for me!
    Be discreet, Don't let a word
    By a single soul be heard,
Favors, to be kind, must be
Ever granted silently.

    Silently, silently
Do the deeds of amity!
    They are alms whose virtue rare
    Dies, when open's to the air!
Would you earn a smile from me?
Win and wear it – silently!

        John Howard Payne
        From <u>Woman's Revenge</u> (1832)
        Published with the play in
        <u>America's Lost Plays</u>, Vol. 6 (Princeton, 1940).

About the Author:

Shirley Sprague has her BS in Education from Wittenberg University, Ohio, with a major in English and minors in Music and History. She received her master's Degree in English from Kent State University in Ohio.

She taught high school English and college English and Research Skills. She and her husband have traveled extensively over the USA and abroad. A widow and mother of four sons, she lives in Elyria, Ohio.

Printed in the USA
CPSIA information can be obtained
at www.ICGtesting.com
LVHW041510130624
783067LV00001B/85

9 781491 742006